Johnny
and the
Light

By: Deriyun McGee

Illustrated by: Angel Dela Pena

ISBN: Softcover   978-1-5245-0064-1
        Hardcover   978-1-5245-0065-8
        EBook   978-1-5245-0063-4

Print information available on the last page

Rev. date: 05/16/2016

To order additional copies of this book, contact:
Xlibris
1-888-795-4274
www.Xlibris.com
Orders@Xlibris.com

Johnny and the Light

By: Deriyun McGee
Illustrated by: Angel Dela Pena

To:
Richard &
Laylah

God bless

Deriyun
McGee

Johnny hates to go to bed at night. Under his sheets he lay with fright. Johnny never sleeps without a light. Because the monsters come out of the closet at night.

So every night Johnny slept with a light. He didn't want the monsters or bed bugs to bite. Johnny feels safe in the light, but there was a night without a light.

Johnny's mom sat on his bed and tucked him in. Johnny asked her to tell him a story with a happy ending.

Johnny's mom read aloud. She told the story of Jesus and how he went to heaven on a cloud. Jesus is the son of GOD and the saviour of men. Jesus came to Earth to wipe away sin. Jesus loves us all no matter the color of our skin.

The devil shows up and scares children at night. The name Jesus will make the devil run away with fright.

Johnny's mom kissed him on the forehead goodnight. She walked out of the room and left on the light. Johnny dosed off and everything was alright.

As Johnny slept, he had sweet dreams. The light shined bright creating a peaceful scene. Suddenly the room became dim because the light bulb flickered.

The light bulb went out! The closet
door slowly opened followed by
evil snickers. Johnny's peaceful
dreams became nightmares. He
was awakened by movements in the
dark and uncomfortable stares!

Johnny was terrified as he looked around his room. He hid under the covers scared the monsters would get him soon!

Then Johnny remembered the story his mom read aloud. About the story of Jesus and how he went to heaven on a cloud. The Son of God has power over men and spirits. Johnny screamed out to Jesus so the monsters can hear it.

Suddenly a light appeared and a voice fell from the clouds. It said, " Peace be with you." Then the room was no longer loud.

Everything suddenly vanished and
the room was without a sound.
Little Johnny fell fast asleep that
night and he didn't need a light.

The End